THE RED RIDER

BY THE SAME AUTHOR:

FOR GROWN-UPS:

THE RED RIDER

Julian Middleton

"It had been snowing for three days and more than two metres had settled on David Tavish's farm. Flakes the size of fifty pence coins wheeled and spun in the frozen air and fell so thickly that if you inhaled too sharply, you could almost choke on them. A great drift had settled against the eastern side of the house and Mr Tavish had been clearing the farmyard twice an hour, trying to keep it clear. Nevertheless the old farmstead, isolated to begin with, was now well and truly cut off from the outside world and the old stone buildings seemed to shiver from a combination of loneliness, chill and fear…"

Mrs McBride clapped her hands together and paused to wipe an imaginary tear from her eye. "Wonderful, wonderful! Michael, you're a born storyteller. A highly effective combination of atmosphere and rising suspense! Remind me again what your story is called?"

"*Silent Night, Bloody Night*," said Michael Flaugherty. He smiled briefly before sitting down. "It's based on the Legend of Tannersley Woods."

"The what, dear?"

"You know," Michael said. "The tale of the Red Rider and all that."

"I can't say I'm familiar." Mrs McBride frowned, apparently searching her memory. "What's all that about then?"

"It's not true!" John Sackley strode across the playing fields, schoolbag slung untidily across his shoulders. "Flaugherty made it up to impress McBride! He always was a swot."

"I thought it had the ring of truth," Steve Moore said, struggling to keep up. "All that stuff about supernatural horsemen and children being kidnapped…you couldn't make it up!"

"What's more, I didn't."

The two boys halted beside the tall hedge that marked the school boundary. Michael Flaugherty grinned at them. "It's all true - every word. I got it from here." He knelt down and pulled a large, leather-bound book from his bag. Steve glanced at the title.

"*Fifty Fearsome Fiends*," he read. "You get that from the library?"

"It belonged to my grandfather," Michael said. "He left it to me in his will." He opened the cover and turned to the contents list. Steve observed that story number twenty-three was entitled *The Legend of Tannersley Woods – The Red Rider*.

"Yeah, so it's a story," nodded John. "Just like I said!"

"No, these are all true accounts." Michael flicked through the pages until he found the story in question. "See? As told by Philip Gourmande to Constable Ronald Pickering, January 1899."

"Hi! What's going on?"

Steve turned at the sound of a female voice.

"This is my sister, Michelle," Michael told them. "I was just explaining to the lads here about the Red Rider."

Michelle pulled a face. "You're obsessed with that story," she said. "Wish you'd just drop it."

It had grown fully dark by the time the little group reached the lights of town and the high street. The sky was clear and filled with cold, bright stars. The coffee house on the corner of Woodrow Road, however, was warm and welcoming.

"The thing is, all you did was rewrite that story by Philip Gourmande and call it your own," John observed. "And now Mrs McBride thinks you're the next James Herbert."

"Yeah, but I made it my own," Michael said. "And I told you, it's not by Gourmande, it's about him. Technically it's by Constable Pickering. In fact he then recounted it to someone else, so absolutely technically the story is by him or her."

"Who's that then?"

"I don't know," Michael grumbled. "That's the point of legends – they get handed down, don't they?" He sipped his coffee and grinned. "Besides, there are no new stories you know, not really new. There are only about seven basic stories and people have been telling and retelling them for thousands of years. Like the conquering hero, the worm that turns, rags to riches, Jason and Goliath and so forth."

Steve was leafing through *Fifty Fearsome Fiends*. "Tell us some more about this Red Rider then," he said. "It sounds cool."

"I'm sick of hearing about it," Michelle promptly groaned. "Make it quick or I might leave."

"What, and walk home by yourself in the cold and the dark?" Michael challenged. Michelle sulked and glanced through the window. Some men were putting up a huge Christmas tree on the nearby roundabout.

"So this fellow Philip Gourmande lived about a hundred years ago," explained Michael, "in, uh, Lancashire I think it was, or it might have been Yorkshire..." He frowned.

"Yorkshire," sighed Michelle.

"Right. He owned a big house in the absolute middle of nowhere on the edge of a forest called Tannersley Woods..."

"How can a forest be called a wood?" John interrupted.

"If it were left to me, it would've been Tannersley Forest," said Michael.

"But it was left to you!" John smirked. "Why didn't you change it when you wrote your own version?"

"John, let him get on with it," muttered Steve. "I'm supposed to be home by six."

John shrugged. Michael swallowed some coffee. "So, it's close to Christmas 1898 and a massive snowstorm moves in and completely cuts the house off from the outside world, just like I read out in class, except I made it a farm, okay? Old Gourmande is left totally isolated and I mean totally isolated. Remember this is the days before phones, cars, snowploughs and stuff."

The other three listened intently.

"After three days, he runs out of firewood, so he has to go into the forest to get some. So there he is chopping away with his trusty axe when he begins to hear something other than the echo from his labours…" Michael paused dramatically. "Something a lot like horse's hooves, coming closer through the trees. Suddenly he looks up and there he is, the Red Rider, a tall figure clad in a long red cloak, tearing past on a huge black horse. There is smoke coming from the horse's nostrils and as it goes past Gourmande sees that beneath the red hood the Rider has a skull for a face."

Michelle shuddered and clutched her hot chocolate.

"But worse is to come, because slung over the horse's back is a large dirty sack and there is clearly something alive and struggling inside…and just as the Rider flashes by, Gourmande hears a voice crying, 'Help, help me please!' from inside…a child's voice, a young girl…"

Michelle jumped up. "That's it, I'm going home!" She hurried out and slammed the door.

"And that's it; the Rider is gone, headed back into the forest with his hapless prey." Michael drained his coffee. "But that isn't the end of the tale, far from it. Old Gourmande is a courageous bloke. He fetches his fastest steed from the stables and follows the Red Rider's tracks deep into the woods, heading further and further into the middle of nowhere. After several hours' pursuit, he comes across a clearing right at the foot of a steep cliff. Here the snow is all trampled and packed down. There is no sign of the Rider or his horse…all Gourmande finds, to his horror, is a little pile of bones in the middle of the clearing – bones that have been picked completely clean." Michael smiled thinly. "Children's bones."

"Well," John said eventually, "that is quite a story. Though it quite clearly never happened."

"Don't be such a cynic," Steve remarked. "The world is full of mysteries."

"It's time my stomach was full of food."

They talked about other things for a short while.

"Are you finished with that?" Michael retrieved his book from Steve and thrust it into his bag. He glanced through the window into the night. "Now, is it my imagination or is it starting to snow?"

The skies had clouded over surprisingly quickly while they had been sitting in the coffee shop, and the stars had been obliterated. As the workmen finished erecting the tree, a scattering of fine flakes drifted down to greet them. Michael grinned at John and Steve. "Reckon it'll snow like it did in 1898?"

"Nope," John said. "See you later!"

"Cracking story, Mike," said Steve. "Try making one up from scratch next time, eh?"

Michael watched them saunter up the high street and shrugged. There was just no impressing some people. Probably, he thought, they had been just as scared as his sister, but reluctant to show it. It was snowing harder as he walked in the opposite direction, rounding the corner and heading along Woodrow Road. Soon he was leaving the town behind and passing empty fields just starting to glisten with frost.

A kilometre or so ahead, he glimpsed the comforting lights of Simonstone, the tiny village where he lived. The glow from the village lights was steadily dissolving into a dreamlike blur as the snow intensified.

Michael wondered how far ahead his sister had managed to get, or whether she had actually arrived home yet. It was a good twenty-minute walk to Simonstone and Michelle was hardly a fast walker. Then again, perhaps she had run the whole way, looking over her shoulder the entire time. Michael grinned to himself. *Fifty Fearsome Fiends* was proving great fun. He had read quite a few of the supposedly true tales contained within his grandfather's book, but none had captured his imagination like the account of the Red Rider, the supernatural kidnapper of young children. A lot of the other stories were rather familiar tales of ghosts and hauntings, not dissimilar to many he had read over the years. The Red Rider was something else again however – so vivid in his mind's eye – so real…

Michael felt a shudder run up his spine as he heard the faint sound of horse's hooves coming toward him through the snow. He stopped walking, suddenly conscious of the weight of the book in his schoolbag, and peered ahead. The noise grew steadily louder and a large silhouette loomed up in the darkness, a big horse with rider bolt upright…

"Good evening!" It was a middle-aged woman, smiling cheerfully. "Wouldn't have set out if I'd known this was coming!" She receded into the darkness, headed toward town. Michael composed himself, heart thudding rapidly, and moved swiftly on.

When he got home, the house was empty and dark. Michael went round closing curtains and turning on lights. At half past five, his mum came in from work. The street was rapidly turning white. Michael waited in the hallway.

"Everything all right, Michael?"

"Mum, we went to the coffee shop and Michelle left well before me but she's still not home and she's not answering her mobile."

"Really?" His mum seemed unconcerned. "No doubt frightened by another of those stories of yours." She hung up her coat. "Well, she probably went round to Kathy's."

Michael relaxed a little. Yes, that was undoubtedly it. Michelle often visited her friend after school. Why hadn't he thought of that? Anxiety was clouding his thoughts. Now the stories were getting to him! He went upstairs, sat on the bed and pulled out the book. Opening the thick leather cover, he studied the faded inscription: *To Laurence, Fondest Regards, P.A.G.*

Michael turned idly to the very back of the book and to his surprise a battered sheet of paper fell out and drifted to the floor. He picked it up, noting its age and fragility, and carefully opened it out. It was a letter.

My Dear Laurence

In the certain knowledge that my time is almost at an end, I entrust this precious First Edition into your care for safekeeping. No doubt many would be flattered to find their story in print – would that it were so in my case! I wish with all my heart that I had not stumbled across the horror that is the Red Rider – or, should I say, that he had not stumbled across me! I cannot vouch for the authenticity of the other tales in this somewhat notorious volume, but be under no illusion, old friend – the Rider exists. He may or may not still haunt the old woods near my home – I cannot say, for I have not glimpsed him since that terrible winter night so long ago! But he is out there somewhere to this very day, I am convinced of it, for the Bringer of Death is not subject to death himself! And when the winter wind blows and the snow falls, the children of this land should fear for their lives!

May God protect you, my friend.

Yours Truly

Philip Anthony Gourmande

12th April, 1956

Michael read the letter several times before folding it and carefully replacing it at the back of the book. Turning to the front again, he studied the inscription. Why hadn't he seen it before? P.A.G. – Philip Anthony Gourmande! Gourmande had actually known his grandfather and bequeathed the book to him, just as his grandfather had passed it on to him in his will!

He flicked through the pages containing the story of the demonic Rider before crossing to the window and drawing back the curtain. It was snowing heavily now and the gardens and rooftops were vanishing. The door opened and his mum entered clutching the phone and suddenly pale.

"I've just spoken to Kathy," she said. "She hasn't seen Michelle today at all."

Minutes later, Michael and his mum drove slowly up the road back to town. The headlights picked out the white road surface and other vehicles' tyre tracks. Michael scanned the dark hedgerows and verges as the wipers repeatedly cleared fresh snow from the windscreen. He had rung his sister's mobile five times. There was no answer.

"Can you think of anywhere else she might be?" Michael's mum braked as a car sped by, passing dangerously close. "Any new friends that you know of?"

Michael shook his head. "No. Just the usual faces. Besides, I'm sure she intended to go straight home."

"Oh dear…" She bit her lip. "I don't like this at all. Why isn't she answering her phone?"

They drove all the way up Woodrow Road to the high street. The coffee shop was just closing; the Christmas tree on the roundabout stood waiting for lights to be added the following day. The town centre was quiet. Michael's mum drove slowly through the silent streets, and the headlights caught thousands of snowflakes whirling and descending. By now Michael had managed to ring most of Michelle's close friends. No one had seen her since school. He rang home, hoping that she may have miraculously arrived, but no one picked up.

"Try Julie's," he suggested. "Carmount Road. Those two tell each other everything."

Julie Hughes, a pretty girl with lots of black hair, had not spoke to Michelle since lunch. She was dismayed to learn that she was missing.

They started back towards Simonstone in near-blizzard conditions; the hedgerows crouched by the roadside had two centimetres of snow resting upon them. The meadows were white. So was his mum, Michael noted.

"Perhaps I had better not waste any more time and phone the police as soon as we're home," she said.

Michael glanced at his watch. "It's only seven," he said, trying to sound reassuring.

"I know. But if something really is wrong, time is of the essence."

They drove into Simonstone in fraught silence, and pulled into the driveway. Despite his hopes to the contrary, Michael found no fresh footsteps on the drive, or melting snow inside the front door. The place was exactly as he had left it.

"What time exactly did she leave the coffee house?"

Michael thought hard. "I'd say it was about quarter past four."

"Could it have been earlier, or a little later maybe?"

"A little either way. Maybe ten or twenty past…"

Michael watched her go to the phone and dial. After a few moments, she said, "Hello, my daughter is missing; no one has seen her since just after four this afternoon."

Intent on listening, Michael was distracted by a loud thump from the ceiling. Frowning, he glanced up the stairs. It sounded like a large piece of furniture being moved and it definitely came from his room! He moved to the bottom of the stairs and placed a hand on the banister.

"Michelle Flaugherty. She's nine. She'll be ten in January."

A second thump, louder than the first, shook the ceiling. Michael's confusion and alarm turned unexpectedly to hope. Perhaps Michelle had come home after all and was up in his room for some reason! He ran up the stairs, taking them two at a time, crossed the landing and pushed open the bedroom door. The light was off. He flicked the switch and something flew across the room and promptly smashed the bulb. Michael just had time to glimpse a large figure beside the bed.

It held his grandfather's book in its hands.

Seconds later the window smashed and freezing air blew in. Michael saw a very tall man in silhouette against the lights of the house behind his own. The man leapt out of the window and plunged into the garden. Below, a horse whinnied. Michael ran to the window and looked down. His heart nearly stopped as he watched a figure all in red leap on to a huge black steed that waited on the snow-covered lawn. Clutching *Fifty Fearsome Fiends* in its hand, it urged the horse around and spurred it toward the back fence. Michael gasped as he beheld a writhing sack strapped across the horse's flanks.

"Michael! Michael, help me!" It was unmistakably his sister's voice, muffled but clearly recognisable. A moment later the horse and rider vaulted the fence into the next garden and vanished into the night.

II

Michael rushed down the stairs, his heart thumping madly, ran past his mum who was still on the phone and down the short corridor that led to the kitchen. Unlocking the back door, he flung it open and dashed into the garden. He stared in shocked bewilderment at the horse's tracks amid the shattered glass from his window. He could place both his feet in each hoof-mark! Following the tracks to the back fence, Michael peered over and saw them continue across the neighbouring garden and down the side of the house.

"Michael, what on earth are you doing?"

He spun round. "Mum, it's the Red Rider! He was in my room; he took the book and he's got Michelle!"

For a moment Michael saw fury cross her face, but he pointed silently up at the broken window and then down into the snow. His mum took several faltering steps into the garden, still clutching the phone, but when she opened her mouth to speak no sound emerged.

"I'll be back!" Michael promised. He climbed over the fence and dropped down. Hurrying across the garden and down the drive, he pursued the horse's tracks out on to Alexandra Street. The street was quiet and deserted. The hoof-marks ploughed up the snow for some considerable distance, interspersed with tyre tracks, leading east toward the outskirts of the village. Michael followed.

Alexandra Street cut a straight path through the heart of Simonstone before shrinking into a much narrower lane and disappearing on to Blackthorpe Moor. Michael pursued the Red Rider for the better part of a kilometre, only hesitating when he reached the point where the last houses receded behind him and the darkness closed in. There were no more streetlamps and fresh snow was already doing its best to cover his quarry's tracks. The moor loomed ahead; it glowed with a pale, eerie light in the snow. Michael caught his breath, torn between going on and turning back.

His mobile rang in his pocket and the shrill tone made him jump.

"Hello?"

"Hey Mike, it's Steve. What you up to?"

Michael told Steve exactly what he was up to. There was an astonished silence. "Where are you exactly?" Steve demanded thereafter.

"I told you; I'm on Alexandra Street, right at the point where it narrows. Just past the last streetlight."
"I'm on my way."

"Bring two torches!"

Fifteen minutes later, Michael and Steve pushed on down the narrow lane as the snow continued to fall. The Rider's tracks were rapidly fading but still discernible thanks to the torchlight.

"It's incredible...unbelievable!" Steve kept shaking his head until he resembled a dog trying to dry itself. "The Red Rider...in your own bedroom!"

"It was definitely him," Michael told him. "I saw him clearly as he rode across the garden. Just like in the book." He fell silent, remembering.

"But why take the book?"

"To cover his tracks. The book proves his existence."

"Not necessarily," said Steve. "It could just be fiction – it doesn't prove anything."

"Well, he undoubtedly thinks it does! Anyway he took Michelle. That's what's important right now."

Steve nodded. He shone his torch down into the snow and stopped abruptly. "Look."

The hoof-marks suddenly veered to the right and vanished. Michael's heart sank. It looked like the animal had vanished into the air! He approached the hedge at the side of the lane and pointed his torch at it. A layer of snow had been dislodged. "He jumped here," he said. "Help me up, would you?"

Steve boosted Michael over the snow-capped hedgerow. He tumbled down the other side and landed in a heap. Still on his knees, he pointed the torch ahead. Beyond the lane there was nothing but empty moor.

Steve dropped down beside him, surprisingly nimbly. He helped Michael to his feet. "The tracks are fading," he observed. "He must be well ahead by now."

Michael nodded. The marks in the snow were little more than shallow depressions. He squinted ahead. "I reckon that's Blackcorner Rocks up there."

"You've got a better sense of direction than me," said Steve.

"Come on, let's keep moving."

They pushed on. The snow was halfway to their knees in some places and a rising wind blew the falling flakes hard in their faces. Michael's phone rang again. "Hi Mum. What? No, I'm with Steve. We're following the tracks across the moor." His mum was practically shrieking in his ear. "We're okay! What did the police say? All right, we'll head back in a minute!"

The signal faded and the connection promptly cut.

"The police are sending a car to the house to take down some more information," Michael said. "Wait 'til they see my bedroom window!"

"There it is."

A tall series of jagged rocks rose from the otherwise featureless landscape not far ahead. They stood out in sharp relief against the white backdrop.

"Blackcorner Rocks," Michael muttered. "Could there be a more joyless place?"

He had some cause to be thankful, however, since the rocks afforded protection from the weather. They overhung in several places and the ground was almost completely free of snow. The wind died and it felt temporarily warmer. The boys paused to recover themselves before making their way through the rocks and emerging on the far side. The blizzard had renewed its intensity as if it too had enjoyed a respite and waited for them.

They found no further trace of the horse and its rider.

"That's it," Steve said. "We have to go back, Mike! Any further and we could end up completely lost. There's nothing out there except thirty kilometres of moor."

"No," Michael said, thoughtfully. "Out there is Ellenhall Wood."

Steve hesitated. "All right, what if it is?"

"The Red Rider lives in the woods and forests; we know this." Michael shone his torch into the night. "That's where he's going – that's where he's taking Michelle." He paused. "Into the trees."

Steve took a deep breath. "Come on, then," he nodded. "At least we'll have some shelter there."

They entered Ellenhall Wood not long after. It was composed in the main of dense pine trees and inside only a scattering of snow had reached the ground. They were once again free of the punishing wind and the night was warmer. But they found no further trace of the Rider. Having plodded through the silent forest for some time, the boys eventually came to a halt beside a giant oak tree that stood incongruously amid the tall pines. Michael dusted snow from a nearby log and sat down.

"I believe the trail ends here," he muttered.

"Best plan now is to head back and tell the police all that we know," Steve said after a moment. "Or better still, call your mum right now."

Michael took out his phone. "No signal.".

Steve checked his mobile also. "Ditto."

Michael gazed through the trees. The image of the hooded demon, caught for the briefest of moments in the glare of his bedroom light, flashed in his mind's eye once more. He shook his head, still scarcely able to believe it. Suddenly the hour in the coffee shop late that afternoon seemed a very long time ago.

"Hey," Steve said unexpectedly, "is that a road up ahead?"

Michael refocussed. Steve had an eagle eye. Some way off through the trees he discerned a kind of thin, pale strip barely covered with snow. As he studied it, he found his heart starting to thud once more and a chill crept into his gut that had nothing do with the air temperature. Michael got to his feet and approached, weaving his way through the trees; Steve duly followed.

It turned out to be a narrow track or path running through the forest, definitely man-made. Trees had been felled here and there, but overall the path was sufficiently protected by the pines to elude most of the snow. Michael glanced left and right.

"I reckon we follow it," he said. "Which way, though?"

"But why?" Steve shrugged. "There's no sign of tracks."

"Instinct."

As Michael hesitated, the deep silence was interrupted by a faint sound in the distance. Michael glanced to his right. "Did you hear that?" Steve shook his head. "Come on – this way."

They made their way cautiously along the path. The light smattering of snow upon it lay undisturbed. Finally Steve said, "What was it you heard, anyway?"

"It sounded like someone chopping wood," Michael answered.

A minute later, the trees began to thin out and shortly thereafter a large rambling stone house loomed up in the darkness. Removed from the protection of the trees, it was covered in snow. Lights burned in several ground floor windows. Michael and Steve approached warily, once more blinded by the blizzard.

"This is the other side of the forest," Michael realised. He frowned. "How can we have got here so quickly?"

"It can't be the other side," said Steve. "We must've turned and reached another edge, so to speak."

The house was clearly very old although it seemed to be in good repair. There were stables to one side and a large courtyard in front. The wind drove the snow across the empty courtyard where it piled up against a wall on the far side.

The boys stood at the entrance which was protected by heavy wooden gates. The right-hand gate stood open. Steve was about to set foot inside but Michael held him back. "Don't you hear that?" he whispered. "Listen…"

Steve strained to hear and now he did hear it – a definite sound of chopping wood from back in the trees. He stared at Michael. "Who would be out felling trees on a night like this?"

"Search me," Michael said nervously. He scanned the trees. "A very keen lumberjack?"

The noise continued to echo from the woods. Michael took out his phone again. There was still no signal. He glanced up at the house. "Maybe we can ring from here," he mused.

"I don't see any power lines," Steve observed. "Or TV aerials, or anything, actually." But Michael was already heading back towards the forest. "Hey! Where are you going?"

"Maybe whoever it is can help us!"

Steve rolled his eyes and hurried to catch up. They followed the now-regular chopping noises for several hundred metres until they came across a narrow clearing where a man stood over a fallen log, hacking away with a huge axe. He stood with his back to the boys, clad in a long overcoat, hood and gloves.

"Excuse me," Michael said. The man whirled around, glaring and clearly startled.

"Who the devil are you?"

"Michael. Michael Flaugherty. We're looking for my sister, Michelle. She's been kidnapped."

"Kidnapped?" The woodsman lowered his axe. "I'm sorry to hear that, Master Flaugherty, but the woods are no place for children at the best of times. You'd best be getting home."

"Not 'til I find my sister!" said Michael. "I can't go back until I do."

The man frowned. "Where have you come from – Tannersley?"

"Simonstone," Michael said. Then he froze. "Where did you just say?"

"Tannersley's the only village within ten miles of here," the woodsman observed. "This place you mention, I've never heard of it."

Michael and Steve looked at each other in disbelief. Fresh alarm gripped Michael's insides. Before he could say anything, their companion wheeled abruptly and stared intently off into the trees. "Hear that?" he muttered. "Been hearing that for the past half hour off and on. Who would be so foolish as to be out riding in this weather?"

"Oh no..." Steve's eyes were suddenly wide. "Please don't tell me..."

The sound of galloping hooves was getting rapidly louder, echoing across the little clearing. Michael and Steve gasped in unison as a great black steed burst through the trees. The cloaked figure that hunched over its neck had a terrifying skull-face.

"My God!" the woodcutter gasped.

The horse drew level and Michael gazed distraught at the sack tied across its back. He fell backwards but the Red Rider reached down, snatched Steve in one outstretched claw and swept him away into the white woods. His cries reverberated among the watchful pines and diminished into silence.

III

Michael struggled to keep up with the woodcutter as he strode back towards the house. He seemed quite panic-stricken and was muttering to himself.

"Slow down!" Michael protested. "I need to talk to you!"

"No time to talk!" the woodsman fired back. "I've a steed in my stables that can outrun the wind and he can surely outrun that devil!"

"No, no, it doesn't play out that way, trust me! I've read the book!"

"What book?" The man glanced over his shoulder without slowing down. "What are you talking about?"

"I'm talking about the Legend of Tannersley Woods, Mr Gourmande!"

Philip Gourmande slowed down and finally stopped just a few dozen paces from the gates of his house. He stared at Michael, clearly thunderstruck. "How do you know my name? What the devil is going on here?"

Michael fought to recover his breath. "I know a lot more than your name," he said. "I have – or I should say had – a book entitled *Fifty Fearsome Fiends*. It's a collection, an anthology of true accounts of ghosts and hauntings. One of them is about the Red Rider who haunts these woods, Mr Gourmande. The book was published in 1901. You gave a copy to my grandfather, Laurence Flaugherty, in 1956. He left it to me last year when he died."

Mr Gourmande's expression changed from bafflement to incredulity before finally resolving into annoyance. "Firstly, I don't know anyone by that name," he began.

"Not yet. But you will."

"Secondly, this is the Year of our Lord 1898. Now you run back to Tannersley, or Simonstone or wherever it is that you come from!" Mr Gourmande hurried through the gates into the courtyard.

"If you pursue the Rider, you won't find him!" Michael warned. "Only the bones of his victims!"

Mr Gourmande ignored him. Michael watched in dismay as he strode across the snowy courtyard toward the stables, unbolted the door and went inside. He swiftly re-emerged with a sleek black steed that tossed its head nervously at the snow. Mr Gourmande climbed up without bothering with a saddle. Bringing the horse over, he looked down at Michael who detected a new curiosity in his gaze.

"Laurence Flaugherty, you say? I know a David Flaugherty. Runs an antique bookshop in the village. Very fond of ghost stories…"

"My great grandfather perhaps," Michael shrugged. "I don't know."

"You know more about the hooded rider, information that may help me catch him?" Michael nodded. "Then climb up here, boy, and let's be on our way!"

Michael clung to Mr Gourmande's back as the black steed thundered through Tannersley Woods. Bereft of a saddle, he bounced painfully up and down. The snow had finally begun to penetrate the trees and accumulate more thickly on the ground. Consequently, they were able to follow the Rider's tracks quite easily.

"So, is it a ghost or a devil, is it alive or dead?" Mr Gourmande demanded.

"I don't know!" Michael shouted over his shoulder. "You saw it for yourself, the same as I did: a skull for a head and clad in a cloak! It preys on children and it lives in the woods!"

"Tannersley Woods?"

"Yes, and others too, I think! Maybe any wood or forest!"

"If it lives in Tannersley Woods, I've never heard of it before!" Mr Gourmande declared.

"You have now, though!"

Mr Gourmande urged the horse on and it picked up greater speed. They rode and rode and the night wore on until finally they approached the foot of a cliff, just as Michael knew they would. His spirits sank as they cantered into a trampled clearing. Mr Gourmande eased the horse to a standstill and looked around.

"You best stay up there, boy," he muttered. "Wish I had thought to bring a lantern."

"Try this." Michael reached into his pocket and produced his torch. He switched it on and handed it to Mr Gourmande, who gaped at the device in amazement.

"What manner of instrument is this?" he gasped.

"Just point it in the right direction!" Michael dismounted and glanced warily about. The clearing was deserted but he already knew what he was looking for. As Mr Gourmande waved the torch around, Michael approached the middle of the cleared space. He looked down.

"Over here," Michael said, quietly.

Together they studied the little pile of tiny bones.

"God in Heaven," whispered Mr Gourmande. "What manner of infernal creature would do such a thing?"

Michael turned away, feeling helpless. It had all played out exactly as he had feared. Somehow he and Steve had entered the world of the Legend of Tannersley Woods, the realm of the Red Rider, and now Steve as well as Michelle had fallen victim to its clutches.

He took a step forward and his foot dislodged something half buried in the snow. Michael bent down and picked it up, suddenly hopeful. It was a torch – and it worked! He shone the piercing beam around the clearing.

"And then there were two…" he murmured.

The beam of light picked out the base of the cliff. He frowned, looking more closely. What at first resembled nothing more than a pool of deep shadow proved to be the mouth of a cave. Michael approached cautiously.

"Over here! Look!"

Mr Gourmande hurried across. The torch revealed a sizeable opening in the cliff-face and hoof marks and other, more human tracks leading inside.

"This night isn't over," announced Mr Gourmande. "Come on, boy! Let's track the demon down!"

The cave mouth led into a narrow but surprisingly high tunnel that maintained a steady course back into the cliff. The ground remained fairly even. Michael was braced for a dramatic encounter at any moment but the minutes passed without incident. The air began to grow warmer and there was a strange odour.

"Sulphur," Mr Gourmande observed. "How strange…."

A dull red glow rose in the distance, becoming progressively brighter. Finally they drew near to the exit and emerged on a rocky hillside high above a landscape both alien and frightening. Mr Gourmande made the sign of the cross and Michael swallowed hard. The hillside was steep and barren. It descended to greet a land of crags and deep valleys without any kind of visible life or vegetation. Bursts of fire rose from vents in the ground and the smell of sulphur was pungent; there was volcanic ash everywhere. Overhead a deep red sky loomed vivid and tempestuous.

"It looks like Mars…" Michael said. Mr Gourmande shook his head uncomprehendingly. They stood for several minutes, surveying the landscape. "We can't go back," Michael said finally. "Michelle and Steve could be down there somewhere."

As if to confirm his thoughts, there was a sudden cry from the mid-distance. It echoed up among the rocks.

"Come on!" Michael began to hurry down the barren hillside, and Mr Gourmande followed. The fumes made them cough. It took them quite some time to reach the bottom. They paused to catch their breath and listened for further sounds without success.

"I'd say it came from over there." Mr Gourmande pointed to a sharp rise about half a kilometre away. Michael nodded. They headed toward it, scrambling over boulders and slipping on slopes of sliding ash. Climbing up the rise itself proved particularly difficult and for every two steps gained they seemed to lose one slipping and sliding. Finally, however, they reached the top and looked over. They swiftly ducked back out of sight.

"I don't believe it…" Michael gasped.

He raised his head more cautiously and looked for a second time. Not too far ahead the land levelled out to create a natural plateau that was as flat as a football field. Michael could see that there was a large hole in the ground toward the middle, big enough to swallow a bus. He fought to control himself as he observed his sister and Steve tied back to back against a pillar of rock, close beside the hole.

The Red Rider sat on his horse a few metres from the children. He was not alone. Michael counted eleven other identical figures, all clad in red and also on horseback, arranged in a circle around the opening. They sat patiently, apparently waiting for something.

Michael felt himself turn ice-cold as a terrible guttural roar rose up out of the ground. He heard the two captives scream. The stench of sulphur grew steadily stronger.

"It's a sacrifice," Mr Gourmande muttered. "Perhaps to a god of some kind."

"We have to get down there!"

"There's twelve of them and two of us, and they're on horseback." Philip Gourmande shook his head. "It'd be suicide."

Michael glanced back toward the cave. "No time to go and get the horse," he said.

Another, louder roar reverberated around the plateau. One of the Riders' horses whinnied anxiously. Michael put a hand across his nose and mouth: the air was increasingly hard to breath. Mr Gourmande did the same.

"We'll have to run for it," Michael said. "We have the element of surprise."

"No. The riders facing this way will see you before you get ten paces. You don't stand a chance." Mr Gourmande held up his torch. "How does this contraption function?"

"It works on batteries." Michael was confused. "This is hardly the time for a science lesson, Mr Gourmande!"

"Oh, but it is. Electrical charge plus sulphuric gas equals boom, lad!"

A minute later, the plan was set. "This will make a story to set your grandfather's hair on end," Mr Gourmande remarked.

"If not actually on fire!" Michael enthused. "Okay – one, two, three, go!"

They stood up together and set off running down the far side of the hill toward the level plateau. A third near-deafening roar issued from the hole in the ground. As they neared the plateau several Riders saw them, just as Mr Gourmande had predicted. They immediately broke away from the circle and set off toward the intruders.

"I'll leave it as late as I can!" Mr Gourmande shouted.

Two further Riders broke away also and joined the pursuit. Michael and Mr Gourmande ran side by side, brandishing their torches as if they were swords. Five Riders charged toward them. As they bore down, Michael veered toward his left away from Mr Gourmande. He did not dare glance back. His lungs burned from inhaling sulphur and he was starting to feel dizzy. The hole was only about ten metres ahead now. The remaining Riders faced away from him. Michelle and Steve turned to look his way and gaped in disbelief and astonishment.

Mr Gourmande held his nerve until the lead Red Rider was almost upon him. The grinning skull-face lurked beneath the hood, eyes black and lifeless. Gourmande threw the torch up in the air as high as he could and dashed away to his right. He caught his pursuers by surprise as he had hoped. They maintained a straight course. Looking round he saw Michael closing in on the chasm. A moment later the torch stuck the ground and exploded. A terrific flash lit up the entire plateau and the blast threw him off his feet and flung him several metres through the air. He landed on his back and a wave of heat seared past. When his vision cleared, Mr Gourmande observed all five Riders lying prone on the ground. The horses were picking themselves up; the Riders did not move.

The distraction worked. The Riders beside the hole turned in the direction of the blast and rode off. Michael dashed up to Michelle and Steve and began untying the ropes that bound them to the pillar of rock. He got Michelle free quite easily. In turn she helped him pick at Steve's bonds. They both shuddered as a succession of primitive howls rose from the pit. Michael glanced briefly into the darkness. He saw nothing.

"It's coming!" Michelle gasped.

Steve's ropes proved harder to untie. "Come on, come on!" He struggled against the ties. At last they were undone.

"Go, go!" Michael shoved them both in the direction of Mr Gourmande. He was fleeing towards the rise; three Riders now pursued him.

The others wheeled back toward Michael. He stood beside the pit and raised the torch.

"The moment of truth," he said to himself. Inhaling a particularly deep lungful of fumes, he threw the torch high into the air above the enormous opening. It sailed up, turning over and over under the angry red sky. Michael chased after the others, dodging between the charging horses, the grinning skulls and outstretched talons. He felt bony fingers scrape his back and fail to grip. Mr Gourmande had reached the hill and was scrambling up. The front Rider was right behind him, reaching out.

A final roar issued from the pit and cut off abruptly as an ear-splitting explosion ripped from the hole in the plateau. A ball of fire blossomed from the depths and billowed out in all directions. Michael dropped to his knees and covered his head in his hands. The ground shook as if a giant had landed from the sky. Cracks spread through the rock. For a few moments, Michael's vision went dim. When he looked up, the first thing he saw was Philip Gourmande on the crest of the rise, gesticulating madly, waving at him to get moving. Michelle and Steve were at the bottom, starting up. Several Riders remained on their mounts and Michael was horrified to see them on fire! They were aflame from head to foot, their horses miraculously untouched. They milled around in confusion.

Michael scrambled to his feet, paused to steady himself and ran toward the edge of the plateau. He dashed past the fallen Riders – their horses had bolted – and the three on fire and clambered up the slope after Michelle and Steve. They all reached the top together.

"We have to get back to the tunnel and get out of here!" Michelle cried.

"Look!" Steve pointed down the far side of the rise. Two of the Riders' horses had ceased running and stood together.

They half-ran, half-fell down the slope towards the horses, which tossed their manes and started but remained stationary as the band of escapees approached. Michael and Michelle climbed on to the first; Mr Gourmande and Steve took the other. As they urged the animals in the direction of the cave mouth, Michael looked back and saw a single flaming Rider crest the rise and start down after them.

"I bet that's the original; the one that kidnapped the two of you," he said grimly.

Michelle turned also and groaned. "He swiped me half way down Woodrow Road," she said. "Came out of nowhere."

"Nowhere is right." Michael urged the horse faster. "Come on!"

It was a difficult journey as they steered their mounts between the boulders and up and down the hills, frequently slipping on piles of ash. Finally they came to the bottom of the much higher hill where the mouth of the cave was just visible some considerable distance above.

"Do we take the horses?" Michael wondered aloud.

"He is!" Mr Gourmande pointed. The Rider was perhaps a quarter of a kilometre behind.

"Point taken!"

In the end the big black horses had no trouble negotiating the hillside and they made much swifter progress than they would have on foot. The cave mouth was quickly at hand and shortly thereafter they were passing through the tunnel.

"Is it still following?" Steve asked.

Michael strained his neck but saw nothing. "No reason to think it won't," he replied.

"When we get out," Mr Gourmande said, "we'll gallop, agreed? Can you handle that, Michael?"

"No choice!"

Minutes later they left the tunnel and re-entered the snow-white woods. Mr Gourmande reached out and stroked the neck of his steed, which had waited patiently. "Follow on, Timber!" he urged.

Soon all three animals galloped through the pines as the snow descended thickly, and their hooves ploughed it up. The fresh night air cleared everyone's throats and lungs. Michelle suddenly screamed. Michael looked back and saw the flaming Rider in full pursuit just a few hundred metres behind. He crackled with hellish fire and black smoke trailed after him.

"How did he catch up so fast?" Steve groaned.

"The speed of the devil!" exclaimed Mr Gourmande. "My house will prove no sanctuary – no earthly door will hold him!"

They charged on through the woods, the Rider all crimson and orange behind them, melting snow from the white trees as he passed. They succeeded in holding him off, however, until the gates of Mr Gourmande's courtyard came into sight.

"What have you got on your property?" Michael asked. "What can we use to fight him?"

"A couple of shotguns," Mr Gourmande said. "Heating oil." He paused. "Also one barrel of very old gunpowder. Highly unstable!" He glanced over at Michael as they rode abreast. "Never go near it, actually."

They swept into the courtyard and Mr Gourmande had the sturdy gates closed and barricaded with planks of wood in a trice. Michelle and Steve led the horses into the stables. Then Mr Gourmande showed Michael the way to an outlying woodshed where a sizeable wooden barrel stood in a far corner, half buried beneath a pile of disused tools.

"I hardly dare move it," Mr Gourmande remarked. He looked around. A wheelbarrow lay upside down nearby.

"That ought to do it," Michael nodded.

As they wheeled the cobweb-strewn barrel out into the yard, the gates shook violently and a shower of sparks sailed up into the night. Moments later, they shook again. Mr Gourmande looked over nervously. "He'll be over in a minute!"

"I'll handle this. Go and sort out the other bit."

Mr Gourmande hurried off and Michael pushed the wheelbarrow as steadily as he dared toward the middle of the courtyard. The gates shook for a third time and one of the planks dropped to the ground. Michael rested the barrow and ran after the woodsman. He found him in the enormous kitchen, loading a double-barrelled shotgun.

"I pray this works," he muttered. "I've got nothing better."

"I pray you're a good shot," Michael told him. Gourmande snapped the shotgun together and raised his eyebrows.

"Never miss!"

Even as he spoke, they heard the gates crash open. Through the windows they saw the Red Rider charge into the courtyard and head straight toward the barrel of gunpowder. He leapt over it, rode to the far side of the yard and dismounted. Then he began walking purposefully toward the house. Mr Gourmande gripped the gun.

"Get behind me."

Gourmande raised the shotgun as the Rider smashed the door open and stalked into the kitchen, aglow with flame like some supernatural beacon. He took aim and closed one eye, but the demon promptly lifted the heavy oak table and flung it effortlessly across the room. It struck Mr Gourmande across the chest and he staggered backwards. The gun went off into the ceiling. Michael threw himself to one side. The table pinned Mr Gourmande to the floor and the Rider closed in.

"Run, Michael!"

Michael grabbed the shotgun and dashed round the far side of the room towards the door. "Over here!" he cried. "You know it's me you want!"

The demon hesitated, glowering, before turning. It sidestepped the fallen table and crossed the kitchen in three long strides. Michael ran outside and dodged out of sight behind the door.

The Red Rider walked slowly across the courtyard, looking left and right. Michael examined the shotgun. Mr Gourmande had loaded two rounds and discharged one accidentally. That left one chance only. Raising the weapon, he sighted along the barrel and took aim. He had never fired a weapon in his life!

His quarry suddenly wheeled around, still a safe distance from the barrel of gunpowder. Michael cursed silently as the Rider stalked back toward him.

"Come and get it, you freak!"

Michelle jumped up and down outside the stables immediately opposite Michael. The Rider duly spun again and bore down upon her with frightening speed. In five paces he stood directly over the wooden barrel.

"*Merry Christmas*," Michael muttered and squeezed the trigger. The shotgun went off and kicked savagely into his shoulder. The barrel of gunpowder exploded and blew the demon to kingdom come.

Philip Gourmande was all right. The boys straightened out his kitchen and Michelle tended to his bruised chest. Afterwards, they got ready to leave.

"Don't forget to say hello to my grandfather," said Michael. "He was a good bloke."

"What shall I tell him?"

"Tell him he's a good bloke!"

They took the two horses that had belonged to the Riders and set off through the woods. Michael hoped he and Steve could remember the way back to their point of entry near Blackcorner Rocks. The snow had long since obscured their tracks.

"So, Mr Gourmande," Michelle said, "that was the Gourmande, from the story?"

Michael nodded. "Definitely."

"So, have we been back in time, or what?"

"I don't know about back in time," Michael mused. He paused. "We're alive and I think stories are alive, and sometimes one life interferes with the other, does that make sense?"

"No."

"Good."

The snow had started to abate and through the trees they could see the sky beginning to brighten. In a remarkably short time, they reached the edge of the forest and left the trees behind. The moors lay ahead shrouded in snow. The clouds had cleared away and the stars were fading. A warm glow was visible to the east. The horses quickened their pace. They reached the rocks.

"So, I'm going to write all this up as a story," Michael announced. "A sequel to the Legend of Tannersley Woods."

"Right," Steve nodded. "It can go in a new anthology and get passed down a generation or two and then it can come back to haunt some unsuspecting juveniles."

"Sounds good! Mrs McBride will love it!"

The children glanced at each other. "Do you honestly think that's a good idea?" asked Michelle. "We almost just got sacrificed, a week before Christmas!"

"Maybe I'll keep it to myself," Michael shrugged. "Maybe I'll write a nice, wholesome story instead." He winked at her.

"Please do that," his sister sighed.

Printed in Great Britain
by Amazon